Humpty Dumpty

Humpty Dumpty sat on the wall.
Humpty Dumpty had
a great fall.

All the king's horses and all the king's men
Couldn't put **Humpty** together again!

One, Two, Three Four Five

One... two... three, four, five,
Once I caught a fish alive.
Six... seven... eight, nine, ten,
Then I let him go again.

Why did you let him go?
Because he bit my **finger** so.
Which finger did he bite?
This **little** finger on my right.

Hey **Diddle** Diddle

Hey diddle diddle,
The cat and the **fiddle,**
The cow jumped over the moon.
The little dog laughed
To see such fun,
And the **dish** ran away with the spoon.

Row, Row, Row your Boat

Row, row, row your boat,
Gently down the stream.
Merrily, merrily, merrily, merrily,
Life is but a dream.

Aaaaahhh...

Row, row, row your boat,
Gently down the stream.
If you see a **crocodile**,
Don't forget to scream.

Round and round the garden
Like a teddy bear...

Join in the fun as these five all-time favourite children's rhymes are brought to life by Wendy Straw's charming illustrations.

Produced by Brolly Books,
Suite 330, 45 Glenferrie Road Malvern Victoria 3144 Australia
Copyright Illustrations ©Wendy Straw and Brolly Books, 2020

£2.99

9 781782 262015

KT-840-358